**Check out Barbara Park's other great books,
listed at the end of this book!**

Junie B. Jones Is a Beauty Shop Guy

BY BARBARA PARK

illustrated by
Denise Brunkus

A STEPPING STONE BOOK™

Random House 🏠 New York

Copyright © 1998 by Barbara Park
Illustrations copyright © 1998 by Denise Brunkus

RANDOM HOUSE and colophon are registered trademarks and A STEPPING STONE BOOK and colophon are trademarks of Random House, Inc. JUNIE B. JONES is a registered trademark of Barbara Park, used under license.

www.randomhouse.com/kids/junieb

Educators and librarians, for a variety of teaching tools, visit us at www.randomhouse.com/teachers

Library of Congress Cataloging-in-Publication Data
Park, Barbara.
Junie B. Jones is a beauty shop guy / by Barbara Park ;
illustrated by Denise Brunkus.
    p.   cm. "A stepping stone book."
SUMMARY: After her first trip to a beauty parlor Junie decides she wants to work there, and she practices on her bunny slippers, her dog, and herself with disastrous results.
ISBN 978-0-679-88931-1 (pbk.) — ISBN 978-0-679-98931-8 (lib. bdg.)
[1. Beauty shops—Fiction.   2. Hair—Fiction.   3. Kindergarten—Fiction.
4. Schools—Fiction.]   I. Brunkus, Denise, ill.   II. Title.
PZ7.P2197Jtwe   1998   [Fic]—dc21   97-49197

Printed in the United States of America   37 36 35 34 33 32 31 30 29

Contents

1/
My Brand-new Different Name

My name is Junie B. Jones. The B stands for Beatrice. Except I don't like Beatrice. I just like B and that's all.

Only guess what? That doesn't even matter anymore! 'Cause I am changing my name to a brand-new *different* name!

It popped right into my head when I waked up this morning!

That's how come I jumped out of bed. And I zoomed to the kitchen to tell Mother and Daddy.

They were sitting at the breakfast table.

"People! People! Guess what? Guess what? I am changing my name to a brand-new different name! And it is the loveliest name I ever heard of!"

Mother was feeding my baby brother named Ollie. Daddy was reading his paper.

They did not pay attention to me.

I climbed up on my chair and shouted my new name real loud.

"PINKIE GLADYS GUTZMAN! MY NEW NAME IS PINKIE GLADYS GUTZ-MAN!"

Just then, Daddy looked at me over the top of the paper. 'Cause *now* he was paying attention!

"Excuse me? Could you run that by me one more time?" he asked. "Your new name is Pinkie Gladys *what?*"

I clapped my hands real happy.

"GUTZMAN!" I shouted very thrilled. "PINKIE GLADYS GUTZMAN! AND SO FROM NOW ON EVERYBODY HAS TO CALL ME THAT. OR ELSE I WILL NOT EVEN ANSWER! OKAY, DADDY? OKAY?"

I hugged myself.

"Isn't it just the cutest name you ever heard of? 'Cause Pinkie is the loveliest color I ever saw! Plus Gladys Gutzman is the snack lady at school. And so who wouldn't want to be named after *that* woman? That's what I would like to know!"

Daddy shook his head.

"I don't know. This doesn't really sound like a good idea to me," he said.

I did a frown at that guy.

"Why, Daddy? How come? How come it doesn't sound good?"

"Well, for one thing, it's much too long," he said. "No one will be able to remember a name as long as that one."

I tapped on my chin.

"Hmm," I said. "Hmm, hmm, hmm."

Then all of a sudden, my whole face got happy.

"Hey! I got it! I got the answer!"

After that, I zoomed to my room. And I got some paper. And I zoomed right back again.

"A name tag! We will make a name tag!" I said. "That way, people can *read* my new name. And they won't even have to remember it!"

I gave the paper to Mother.

"Write it down! Write it down! Write my

new name on this paper! Then we can pin it right on my clothes!"

Mother did a frown at Daddy. "Way to go, Ace," she said, kind of mumbling.

After that, she wrote my new name on the paper. And she pinned it to my p.j.'s.

I danced all around the floor.

"PINKIE GLADYS GUTZMAN! MY NAME IS PINKIE GLADYS GUTZMAN!" I sang real joyful.

Mother and Daddy didn't say any words. They just kept on looking at me.

Finally, Daddy got up from the table.

"Well...gotta go," he said. "I've got an appointment to get a haircut."

Mother springed out of her chair. She grabbed Daddy by his shirt.

"Oh no you don't. You *can't*," she said. "I have an appointment to take Ollie to the doctor this morning, remember? If you need to get your hair cut, you're going to have to take *you-know-who* with you."

I tapped on her.

"Gutzman," I said. "The name is Pinkie Gladys Gutzman."

Daddy runned his fingers through his hair. Then he did a big sigh. And he told me to hurry and get dressed.

I jumped way high in the air.

"HURRAY!" I shouted. "HURRAY! HURRAY! PINKIE GLADYS GUTZMAN IS GOING TO THE BARBER SHOP WITH HER DADDY! AND SHE REALLY ENJOYS THAT PLACE!"

After that, I twirled and twirled all over the kitchen. Only too bad for me…'Cause I accidentally twirled into the refrigerator and the stove and the dishwasher.

I got knocked on the floor.

My head made a loud clunking sound.

I felt it real careful.

"Good news," I said. "No damage."

After that, I jumped back up.

And I ran to get dressed for the barber shop.

2/ Meeting Maxine

Me and Daddy drove in the car a real long time.

It was not that enjoyable.

"Are we there yet? How come we're not there? Are we lost? Huh, Daddy? Did you lose us?" I asked.

Just then, Daddy pulled into a parking lot.

"Hey! We're there! We're there!" I hollered very thrilled.

I looked through the window.

"Yeah, only here's the problem. I don't even recognize this place. 'Cause this is not your regular barber shop."

Daddy got me out of my seat belt.

"This is a different barber shop," he explained. "Someone at work recommended it. Only it's not actually a barber shop. It's more of what you'd call...well, okay...it's a *beauty* shop."

My eyes got big and wide at that guy.

"A BEAUTY SHOP? OH BOY! 'CAUSE I LOVE BEAUTY SHOPS EVEN MORE THAN BARBER SHOPS!"

I jumped up and down and all around.

"HEY, EVERYBODY! MY DADDY IS GOING TO A BEAUTY SHOP! MY DADDY IS GOING TO A BEAUTY SHOP!"

"Shh, Junie B.! Please!" said Daddy.

"You *have* to be on your best behavior in this place. I mean it. No acting crazy."

I smoothed my jacket very proper.

"Yeah, only I don't even know what you're talking about," I said. "I never acted crazy in my whole entire career."

After that, I skipped very happy through the beauty shop door.

There was a lady behind a counter.

Her face had big, shiny red lips on it.

"Name, please?" she said.

"Robert Jones," said Daddy.

I stood on my tippytoes.

"Yeah, only he has other names, too," I told her. "'Cause some people call him Bob. And some people call him Bobby. Plus today my mother called him Ace."

The lady looked over the counter at me.

"And what is *your* name?" she asked.

I quick took off my jacket and showed her my name tag.

"Pinkie!" I said. "My name is Pinkie Gladys Gutzman! 'Cause I just thought of that cute name this morning! And it is adorable, I think!"

The lady looked funny at me.

She didn't ask any more questions.

Pretty soon, a different lady walked up. And she shook my daddy's hand.

"Hello. I'm Maxine and I'll be cutting your hair today," she said real nice.

My eyes popped right out at that woman! 'Cause she was wearing a name tag! Just like me!

"MAXINE! HEY! MAXINE! LOOK DOWN HERE! I HAVE ON A NAME TAG, TOO!" I hollered.

Maxine ruffled my hair.

"Pinkie Gladys Gutzman, huh?" she said. "Well, Pinkie Gladys Gutzman...since you're already wearing a name tag, I guess that means you should be my helper today."

"YES!" I yelled. "'CAUSE I ALREADY KNOW HOW TO BE A HELPER! ON

ACCOUNT OF SOMETIMES I HELP MY GRAMPA MILLER FIX STUFF. AND LAST WEEK WE FIXED THE UPSTAIRS TOILET! AND I GOT TO TOUCH THAT BIG BALL THAT FLOATS ON TOP!"

Maxine laughed.

"Wow…a helper with plumbing experience. This must be my lucky day," she said.

After that, she holded my hand. And me and her took Daddy to the sink.

Then Maxine washed Daddy's hair. And she let me hold the fluffy towel.

I holded it real tight in my arms.

"Look, Maxine! Look at me holding the fluffy towel! See how good I am doing? I am not even letting it touch the floor!"

Only too bad for me. Because just then, my nose got some itchy fuzzies in it. And I started to sneeze.

"AH...AH...ACHOO!"

I sneezed right into the fluffy towel.

It was soft as a feather.

That's how come I wiped my itchy nose on that softie thing. Plus also I blowed a teeny bit.

Maxine made a face.

"Yeah, only you don't have to worry. 'Cause I'm not even contagious," I told her.

Then I gave her the fluffy towel to dry Daddy's hair. But Maxine said, "No, thank you." And she dried Daddy's hair with a different fluffy towel.

After that, all of us went to her giant spinny chair.

"HEY! I LOVE THIS KIND OF CHAIR!" I said real excited.

I climbed up there zippity quick.

14

"SPIN ME! SPIN ME! SPIN ME!" I hollered.

Daddy leaned close to my ear. His face did not look pleasant.

"Get *dowwwwwwn*," he whispered very chilling.

I got down.

Maxine patted my head.

She gave me a broom.

It was big and wide.

"Here, helper. You can sweep your daddy's hair as I'm cutting it," she said.

"Yes!" I said back. "'Cause I am excellent at this appliance, I believe!"

After that, I held the broom real tight in my hands. And I runned up and down the floor.

"Look, Maxine! Look at me sweeping! See me? See how fast I am?"

Only too bad for me.

'Cause just then, a lady didn't get out of my way.

And she walked right in front of my big, wide broom.

And her feet got sweeped.

"OW!" she hollered. "OW! OUCH! OW!"

Daddy runned over and snatched my broom away. 'Cause I wasn't the helper anymore, apparently.

After that, he gave Maxine lots of dollars.

And he took my hand.

And me and him rushed right out of that place.

3/ **Practicing**

Daddy drove me home in the car.

I kept on sniffing the air.

"You smell like a lovely woman," I said.

Daddy wasn't that friendly.

"It's the hair gel," he grouched.

I sniffed some more.

"Mmm. I love that smelly hair gel," I said. "Plus also I love sweeping and holding the fluffy towel. And so maybe I might be a beauty shop guy when I grow up."

"Wonderful," said Daddy.

"I know it is wonderful!" I said. "And here's another wonderful thing. I already have a name tag and a towel and a broom and some scissors! And so I am all set to go to work, probably!"

Just then, Daddy quick pulled the car to the curb.

"No, Junie B. No. You're *not* all set to go to work," he said. "You don't just pick up some scissors and start cutting hair. Do you understand? Working in a beauty shop takes years and years of practice."

"Yeah, only I already know that," I said. "I already know it takes years and years of practice."

"Years and years and *years*," said Daddy.

I did a huffy breath at him. "I already know that, I told you," I said again.

After that, I leaned back in my seat. And

I thinked about the years and years of practice.

Finally, I did a big sigh.

I would have to get started right away.

Daddy pulled the car into our driveway.

I runned inside my house zippity quick.

"I'M HOME!" I hollered. "I'M HOME FROM THE BEAUTY SHOP!"

Mother runned out of baby Ollie's room.

"Shh! I just put your brother down for his nap," she said.

I stood there for a minute.

'Cause that woman just gave me a sneaky idea, that's why.

I did a fake yawn.

"Hmm. I need a nap, too, I think," I said. "'Cause that beauty shop got me all tired out."

I walked to my bedroom.

"Well, nightie night. Don't let the bed-bugs fight," I said.

Mother followed me.

Her face looked suspicious.

Suspicious is the grown-up word for *I think maybe you might be fibbing.*

"Whoa, whoa, whoa. Hold on there a second," said Mother. "I thought you hated naps."

"I do," I said. "I do hate naps. But today I worked at the beauty shop. And that job got me pooped, I tell you."

After that, I closed my door. And I got under my covers.

Mother peeked in at me.

I did a fake snore.

Then I waited and waited till she closed the door again.

I stayed in bed till it was safe.

Then finally, I tippytoed to my desk.

And I opened the top drawer real quiet.

I searched my hands all around that thing.

Then all of a sudden my heart got very pumpy!

'Cause my hands felt what they were looking for!

And their name is my bestest shiny scissors!

4/ Snipping, Snipping, Snipping

I opened and closed my shiny scissors real fast.

"Now I can start my years and years of practice!" I whispered very thrilled.

I skipped to my bed where my stuffed animals sit. 'Cause I needed volunteers, of course.

"Who wants to go first?" I asked my animals. "Who wants to get their fur trimmed at my beauty shop?"

My bestest elephant named Philip
Johnny Bob raised his foot.

"*I do! I do!*" he said.

I hugged him very tight. 'Cause that guy
is always a good sport, that's why.

I picked him up and put him in my
beauty chair.

I sat him on lots of pillows so he would
be tall.

Then I kept on looking and looking at his fur.

"Yeah, only here's the problem," I said. "Your fur is made out of softie gray velvet. And softie gray velvet is short and smoothie. And so I can't even trim you."

Philip Johnny Bob did a sad sigh.

I patted his head and put him back on the bed.

Just then, I accidentally stepped on something.

I looked on the floor.

And guess what?

It was my slippers that look like bunnies!

"Us! Us! Trim us!" they said real squealy.

"Hey, yeah! 'Cause you have the beautifulest long white fur I ever even saw! And so you guys will be perfect, probably!"

I quick picked them up and put them in my beauty chair.

After that, I skipped all around them. And I snipped their long white fur.

I singed a lovely song.

It is called "Snipping, Snipping, Snipping Their Long White Fur."

It was the funnest fun I ever even had.

After I got done, I holded them up to the mirror so they could see theirselves.

They did not smile.

"*We're baldies*," they said real soft.

I did a big breath at those guys.

"Yeah, only I already know you are baldies. But that is not my fault. 'Cause you kept on wiggling while I was trimming you," I said.

I petted their heads very nice.

"Don't worry," I whispered. "'Cause

bunny fur probably grows back, probably. I'm almost positive, sort of."

Then I hugged them real gentle. And I throwed them under my bed.

'Cause I didn't want Mother and Daddy to see them, that's why.

After that, I got in bed and did a sigh.

This job was going to take more practice than I thought.

5/ Teddy and Tickle

My bunny slippers didn't grow their fur back.

I peeked at them the whole entire weekend. Only no fur growed at all. Not even a teensy fuzzy.

On Monday—at school—I didn't feel like playing at recess.

My bestest friend named Grace put her arm around me.

"What's wrong, Junie B.?" she said. "How come you don't want to play today?"

I hanged my head real glum.

"'Cause bunny fur doesn't grow back, that's why," I said. "Only who knew? And so now I can't be a beauty shop guy when I grow up, probably. And that was my hopes and dreams."

That Grace's eyes got big and wide at me.

"Hey! Me, too!" she said. "Being a beauty shop guy is my hopes and dreams, too! My aunt Lola owns her very own beauty shop. And she already said I could be a shampoo girl!"

Just then, my other bestest friend named Lucille started fluffing her fluffy hair.

"When I grow up, I'm going to be a *client*," she said. "A client is the person who goes to the beauty shop and spends a small fortune."

She took a little brush out of her purse.
And she started brushing her hair.

"See how shiny my hair is? It's soft
and silky, too. Soft and silky and well-
conditioned."

She shaked it all around in the air.

"A woman's hair is her crowning glory,"
she said. "Want to feel it? Huh? Do you?"

After that, she shaked her hair all around in the air.

"You're getting on my nerves," I said.

Just then, that Grace clapped her hands real loud.

"Junie B.! Junie B.! I just thought of something! Maybe Aunt Lola will let *you* be a shampoo girl, too! And so both of us can be shampoo girls together!"

I did a gasp.

"Really, Grace? Do you really think she would? Really, really, really?"

Then I hugged that Grace as tight as I could.

'Cause guess what?

My hopes and dreams was back!

After I got home from school, I runned to my room speedy quick.

I grabbed my fuzzy teddy off my bed. And I zoomed to the bathroom.

My grandma Helen Miller shouted hello at me. She was in the nursery with my baby brother named Ollie.

"HELLO TO YOU, TOO!" I shouted back. "ONLY HERE'S AN IMPORTANT MESSAGE! 'CAUSE RIGHT NOW I AM SHUTTING THE BATHROOM DOOR. ON ACCOUNT OF THAT IS CALLED PRIVACY, MADAM!"

After that, I locked the door real secret. And I filled the sink with water.

Then I dunked Teddy up and down. And I put shampoo on that guy.

I singed a happy song. It is called "Dunking Teddy Up and Down and Putting Shampoo on That Guy."

Only too bad for me. 'Cause pretty soon,

Teddy's head got soaky wet with water. And he couldn't hold it up that good.

It flopped all around his neck.

I stood him up in the sink. He was a giant sog ball.

I felt sickish inside my stomach.

That's how come I wrapped him in a towel. And I hurried up back to my room.

After that, I patted his sog ball head real gentle. And I throwed him under the bed with my slippers.

I hanged my head real gloomy.

"Darn it," I said. "I am not a good shampoo girl, either. And so now I can never work at Aunt Lola's with that Grace, probably."

Just then, my dog named Tickle scratched at my door.

"Go away, Tickle," I said. "I am not in a playing mood."

But he kept on scratching and scratching.

I opened the door a teeny crack.

"I said to go away. Don't you even understand *language?*"

Only too bad for me. 'Cause Tickle springed right up. And he knocked open the door. And he runned into my room.

He zoomed around and around in circles.

Then finally, he got dizzy and pooped. And he flopped on my rug.

I looked closer at that fellow.

"Hmm," I said. "Your fur is kind of tan-gly and matty. Only I never actually noticed that before."

I tapped on my chin.

"Maybe you should come to my beauty shop for a trim. 'Cause I already had practice. And so I can do better this time, I believe."

I did more thinking.

"Hey, yeah! And here's another good thing. Dog fur grows back. Right, Tickle? And so what do we have to lose? That's what I would like to know!"

I zoomed to my desk and got my shiny scissors.

Then I hurried back to Tickle.

And I gave him a hug.

And I trimmed his tangly, matty fur.

6/ The Trouble with Tickle

Tickle did not turn out that professional.

His fur was choppy and moppish. Plus his tail was a teeny stubby.

I tried to push him under my bed. But he wouldn't even go.

"Yeah, only you *have* to go under there, Tickle. Or else Mother and Daddy will see your fur. And I will be in trouble."

Just then, I heard feet walking in the hall. Oh no!

It was Mother!

She was home from work!

I runned around real upset.

"Hide, Tickle! Hide! Hide!" I said.

Just then, I saw my fuzzy pink sweater!

I grabbed it out of my closet and throwed it on Tickle speedy fast!

Also, I grabbed my favorite hat with the devil horns. And I plopped it on his head.

All of a sudden, Mother opened my door. I backed up from her.

"H-h-hello," I said kind of nervous. "How are you today? I am fine. Plus Tickle is fine, too."

I did a gulp.

"He is wearing clothes, apparently," I said.

Just then, Mother walked to Tickle real slow. And she took off his hat.

That is how come I quick runned out of my room. And down the hall. And outside into the yard.

'Cause I didn't want to be there when the sweater came off, of course!

Mother chased me all over my yard.

That woman is speedier than she looks.

She caught me by my arm and marched me into the house.

After that, she sat me in a chair. And she said my *goose is cooked, young lady.*

Goose is cooked means that your goose is in big trouble. Only I don't actually have a goose. Only that was not the time to mention it, probably.

Just then, my Daddy came home from work.

Mother tattletaled to him about Tickle.

Then both of them hollered a lecture at me.

It was called *What in the World Has Gotten into Me, Young Lady? Do I Not Even Have Good Sense? And Do They Have to Watch Me Every Single Minute?*

After they finished yelling, Mother put me in my room. And she took away my scissors forever.

And here's the worstest part of all.

After dinner I had to take a bath and go right back to bed.

Mother kissed me on my cheek.

It was not that sincere.

"Yeah, only I am not even tired yet," I said. "And so maybe I should watch *Wheel of Fortune,* perhaps."

Mother shook her head.

"No way. No TV," she said. "If you're not tired, you can lie here and think about what you did today."

After that, she shut my door and walked away.

I did a huffy breath at her.

"Yeah, only I don't even *have* to think about what I did today. 'Cause I already *thinked* about it, that's why," I whispered to just myself.

Then I did a teeny smile.

"And guess what else? I think I am making progress."

7/ The Terriblest Trouble

The next morning I was very cheered up.

'Cause I knew what went wrong with Tickle!

Tickle has dog hair! And dog hair is harder to cut than people hair! 'Cause people hair is much more tamer!

I runned to the mirror and looked at my people hair.

"I bet I can cut *this* kind of hair just perfect," I said.

Just then, I heard the front door open.

It was my grampa Frank Miller! He was here to babysit me before school.

I runned and kissed that guy hello.

Then I zoomed right back to my room. And I hollered a message down the hall.

"DON'T COME IN MY ROOM, OKAY, GRAMPA? 'CAUSE I WANT TO GET DRESSED ALL BY MYSELF TODAY! AND I DON'T EVEN NEED ANY HELP!"

After that, I shut my door real tight. And I hurried to my desk.

'Cause guess what?

Extra scissors! That's what!

They were in my middle drawer where I keep them.

I opened and closed them real fast.

Then I skipped to my dresser.

And I combed my bangs silky smooth.

And I snipped their ends right off!

I peeked at myself kind of nervous.

And guess what?

I wasn't even ruined!

I smiled real thrilled.

"I *knew* I could do this! I knew it! I knew it! All I needed was practice!"

After that, I snipped some more bangs. Plus, I snipped some sides. And some top. And some back.

After I was finished, I looked in the mirror again.

I did a teeny frown.

"Hmm. My bangs do not look even-steven," I said.

That's how come I tried to even them up.

Only those dumb things kept getting tiltier and tiltier.

Finally, I got fusstration inside me. And I

took a whole big hunk. And I cut them right off.

"Ha ha! So there!" I said.

I put down my scissors and looked at myself.

I did a gasp.

Oh no! My hair was sticking out all over the place!

"Sprigs!" I said. "I got sprigs!"

That's how come I started to cry. 'Cause sprigs are shortie little sticklets. And they are not attractive, I tell you.

Just then, I heard a knock on my door.

"Junie B., honey? You all right in there?" asked my grampa. "Okay if I come in?"

"NO! NOT OKAY!" I hollered. "I AM STILL GETTING DRESSED! AND SO PLEASE GO BACK TO WHERE YOU CAME FROM!"

Grampa Miller laughed.

"Okay, okay. I get the message," he said. "I'll go make you a sandwich. You'd better hurry up, though. I've got to do some errands, so I'm driving you to school today."

His feet walked back to the kitchen.

I sat down on my bed real upset.

'Cause sprigs is the terriblest trouble I ever even saw.

8/ Hats

I didn't know what to do.

How could I even go to school? 'Cause everyone would see my sprigs! And they would laugh and laugh!

That is how come I couldn't stop crying.

Only all of a sudden, a miracle happened. And it is called *I spotted my hat with the devil horns.*

It was sitting on my desk right where Mother left it. And that hat gave me a good idea!

I quick picked it up and put it on my head.

And guess what?

It hided my sprigs!

"Hey! If I wear this to school, no one will even see my hair!" I said real relieved.

Only just then, I did a teeny frown.

"Yeah, only what if I'm playing on the playground...and somebody steals my devil horn hat off my head? Then everyone will see my sprigs. And they will laugh and laugh."

I thought real hard.

"Hmm," I said. "Maybe I can wear *two* hats. That way, if somebody pulls off one hat, I will still have *another* hat left."

I spotted my shower cap. It was lying on my chair.

I put it on under my hat.

"Yeah, only what if I'm playing on the

playground...and somebody pulls off my devil horn hat...and then they pull off my shower cap, too? Then everyone will see my sprigs. And they will laugh and laugh."

I tapped on my chin.

"*Three* hats!" I said. "I will wear three hats to school! 'Cause that will give me a whole extra hat of protection!"

I opened my bottom drawer and found my ski mask. 'Cause ski masks hide your whole entire everything!

I put the ski mask on my head. Then I put on my shower cap. And my hat with the devil horns.

I looked at myself in the mirror.

"Now nobody can see anything! Not even my nose!"

After that, I got dressed. And I skipped real happy to the kitchen.

Grampa Miller's eyes popped out at me.

"Whoa, whoa, whoa! You can't go to school looking like that," he said.

That's how come I had to tell him a teensy beansy fib.

"Yeah, only today is crazy hat day. And my teacher said we can wear however many hats we want," I said.

Grampa Miller scratched his head.

Then he watched me eat my sandwich through my mouth hole.

And he drove me to school.

I skipped into Room Nine very joyful.

I sat down at my table next to Lucille.

"Hello," I said. "It's me. It's Junie B. Jones. See me, Lucille? See me? I am wearing an attractive hat assortment."

Just then, a meanie boy named Jim pointed and shouted.

"HEY, EVERYBODY! LOOK AT LOONEY B. JONES! WHAT A GOONIE BIRD! he shouted.

Then all of a sudden, he speeded across

the room! And he grabbed my devil horn hat right off my head!

All of Room Nine laughed and laughed.

'Cause they saw my shower cap, of course!

Only lucky for me, because just then my teacher hurried up into the room. And she took control of people.

Her name is Mrs.

She has another name, too. But I just like Mrs. and that's all.

Mrs. grabbed my hat from that meanie Jim. And she gave it back to me.

Then she yelled at all the children. And she took me into the hall.

Mrs. bended down next to me.

"Okay, kiddo. What's the story here?" she asked.

I rocked back and forth on my feet.

'Cause I didn't want to tell her the story here, that's why.

"Yeah, only I don't actually know what you are referring to," I said real soft.

"The *hats,* Junie B. What's the story with the hats?"

Finally, I did a big breath. And I told her the story.

The Story with the Hats
by
Junie B. Jones

"Once upon a time there was a little girl named Pinkie Gladys Gutzman. And she was practicing to be a beauty shop guy. Only too bad for her. 'Cause her stupid dumb bangs kept on getting tiltier and tiltier. And that's how come she had to cut them off. And now she wishes she was never even Pinkie. And that is all the details I would like to share with you at this time."

I did a big breath.

"The end."

Mrs. put her hands on my shoulders.

"Junie B.? Honey? Are you telling me that you cut your bangs off? Is that what this is about?"

I did not answer her.

Then all of a sudden, Mrs. took off my

ski cap. And I didn't even know she was going to do that!

"No," I hollered. "Don't!"

Only it was too late.

Mrs. saw my hair.

She hugged me real tight.

"Oh, Junie B.," she said. "What happened?"

I started to cry all over again.

"Sprigs," I said. "Sprigs happened."
After that, Mrs. gave me some tissues.
And me and her sat down on the floor.
And we figured out what to do.

9/ Learning a Lesson

Finally, Mrs. put my devil horn hat back on my head.

"Here," she said. "This will be the only hat you'll need to wear today. I promise."

After that, we went back into Room Nine. And Mrs. told a teensy beansy fib.

"Boys and girls...may I have your attention, please? Junie B. is starting to get the sniffles. And so I'm going to let her wear her hat in class."

She looked at that meanie Jim.

"All day, Jim. She's going to wear it all day. And no one is to touch it," she said. "Not *anyone*."

I jumped out of my seat.

"Yeah, Jim. You can't even touch it with your baby little pinkie finger. Right, Mrs.? Right? Right?"

"Right," said Mrs.

"Not even at recess. Right, Mrs.? Right?"

Mrs. sucked in her cheeks. "Yes, Junie B. Right."

"And not when I'm getting a drink at the water fountain. And not when I'm bending down to tie my shoe. And not when I'm walking to the pencil sharpener. And not when I'm just plain sitting in my chair. And not when I'm working in my workbook. And not when I'm practicing my alphabet. And not when—"

"Okay, okay. We get the picture!" said Mrs.

I smoothed my dress.

"All rightie then," I said real nice.

After that, I sat in my chair.

And I worked in my workbook.

And I played at recess.

And I went to the water fountain.

And no one touched my hat.

After school, Daddy came to Room Nine to get me.

I was surprised to see that guy.

"Daddy! Daddy! I didn't even know you were coming to get me today! And so this day turned out better than I thought!"

Daddy stared at my hat.

All of a sudden, my stomach did not feel good about this situation.

He reached out and took it off my head.
Then he quick closed his eyes.

"Lovely," he said.

After that, he picked me up. And he
carried me to the car.

I tapped on him.

"Did you really mean it is lovely? Or was that a little joke?" I asked kind of nervous.

Daddy didn't answer my question.

Instead, he buckled me in my seat belt. And we started to drive.

We drove and drove for a real long time.

Finally, we pulled into a parking lot.

I looked out the window.

"Daddy! Hey, Daddy! It's the beauty shop! The beauty shop with Maxine!" I said.

Daddy took me right inside.

And guess what?

Maxine was waiting for me!

She did a smile.

"Hmm. Looks like someone gave herself a little trim," she said.

I felt shy of her.

"I didn't turn out even-steven," I said kind of soft.

Maxine ruffled my hair.

Then she put me in her giant spinny chair. And she sprayed my hair with water.

After that, she snipped and snipped and snipped.

Finally, she put gel on my hair. And she blowed me dry.

I looked at myself in the big mirror.

"Hey! What do you know! No more sprigs!" I said real delighted. "How did you do that, Maxine? How did you do that?"

Maxine winked at Daddy.

"Years of practice," she said.

Daddy leaned close to my face.

"Years and years and *years*," he said.

After that, he lifted me down from the chair.

And he gave Maxine lots more dollars.

And me and him drove home again.

After we got to my house, Daddy came into my room with me.

He took my extra scissors off my desk. And he put them in his pocket.

"Sorry, Daddy. Sorry I cut my own hair," I said.

He did a sigh.

"I know you're sorry, Junie B.," he said. "I just hope you learned a lesson from all of this."

"I *did,* Daddy. I did learn a lesson. I mean it. I mean it. I mean it."

Daddy kissed my head.

'Cause that guy still loves me, that's why.

After he left my room, I looked at my hair some more.

It was the cutest hair I ever even saw.

Just then, my whole face lighted up.

"Hey! *I'm* the one who got this haircut started. And so maybe I can be a beauty shop guy after all!" I said real thrilled.

I tapped on my chin.

"Yeah, only what happens when I grow up and I have to practice some more? What will I use to cut with?"

I looked at my desk very curious.

Then I tippytoed over there real quiet. And I opened my bottom desk drawer.

I searched my hands all around that thing.

Then all of a sudden, I smiled kind of sneaky.

'Cause guess what?

More extra scissors.

Books are my very
FAVORITE things
in the whole world!
I have *lots* of funny
stories to share!
Laugh out loud
with books
like these. . . .

BARBARA PARK

Junie B. Jones
Smells Something
Fishy

BARBARA PARK

Junie B. Jones
Is (almost)
a Flower
Girl

Junie B.'s Sticker Scrapbook Sensation to Spark Your 'Magination!
(Psst! And It's FREE!)

Junie B. Jones

Do You Want . . .

- a special book to save your favorite Junie B. stickers from the new foil-covered paperbacks?
- a perfect place to paste and draw your memories from this year?
- lots of happy, creative scrapbook tips from Junie B.?

YES! YES! YES!

(You can get it FREE at participating retailers and online at www.randomhouse.com/junieb)

Here are some of Junie B.'s favorite photos from her *own* sticker scrapbook!

Bestest Good Friends!

Uh-oh! I'm in Trouble!

464

RANDOM HOUSE
CHILDREN'S BOOKS

Wowie wow wow!
I'm so glad you're my pal!
Let's play at my Web site
I'll meet you there now!

www.randomhouse.com/kids/junieb

Junie B. has a lot to say . . .

the baby's room
Mother and Daddy fixed up a room for the new baby. It's called a nursery. Except I don't know why. Because a baby isn't a nurse, of course.
• from *Junie B. Jones and a Little Monkey Business*

school words
After that, the mop got removed from us. *Removed* is the school word for snatched right out of our hands.
• from *Junie B. Jones and Her Big Fat Mouth*

rules
Me and Mother had a little talk. It was called—*no screaming back off, clown.* Only I never even heard of that rule before.
• from *Junie B. Jones and the Yucky Blucky Fruitcake*

her baby brother
His name is Ollie. I love him a real lot. Except I wish he didn't live at my actual house.
• from *Junie B. Jones and That Meanie Jim's Birthday*

. . . about everything and everybody . . .

saving a seat
Saving a seat is when you zoom on the bus. And you hurry up and sit down. And then you quick put your feet on the seat next to you. After that, you keep on screaming the word "SAVED! SAVED! SAVED!" And no one even sits next to you. 'Cause who wants to sit next to a screamer? That's what I would like to know.
• from *Junie B. Jones Loves Handsome Warren*

twirling
I twirled and twirled all over the kitchen. Only too bad for me. 'Cause I accidentally twirled into the refrigerator and the stove and the dishwasher.
• from *Junie B. Jones Is a Beauty Shop Guy*

cribs
A crib is a bed with bars on the side of it. It's kind of like a cage at the zoo. Except with a crib, you can put your hand through the bars. And the baby won't pull you in and kill you.
• from *Junie B. Jones and a Little Monkey Business*

. . . in Barbara Park's
Junie B. Jones books!

ideas

Just then, I smiled real big. 'Cause a great idea popped in my head, that's why! It came right out of thin hair!

• from *Junie B. Jones Is a Party Animal*

punishment

Grounded, young lady is when I have to stay on my own ground. Plus also, I can go on the rug.

• from *Junie B. Jones Is Not a Crook*

apologies

A 'pology is the words *I'm sorry*. Except for you don't actually have to mean it. 'Cause nobody can even tell the difference.

• from *Junie B. Jones and Some Sneaky Peeky Spying*

school

Kindergarten is where you go to meet new friends and not watch TV.

• from *Junie B. Jones and the Stupid Smelly Bus*